TO MY GOD-FATHER THEO
UP IN HEAVEN

-JAYCE

JAKE & JAYCE

JAYCE: DADDY, WHAT'S A DREAM?

JAKE: A DREAM IS WHEN YOUR IMAGINATION TAKES OVER YOUR BRAIN AND ANYTHING BECOMES POSSIBLE.

JAYCE: REALLY?! I HOPE I CAN DREAM TONIGHT!

JAKE: MAYBE YOU WILL. NOW GO TO SLEEP, YOU HAVE SCHOOL IN THE MORNING.

JAKE & JAYCE

JAKE: SCHOOL'S BEEN CANCELED TODAY,
JAYCE. IT'S JUST ME, YOU AND THAT PLANE
OUTSIDE. PUT ON YOUR GEAR, GRAB YOUR
BAG AND LET'S GO!

JAKE & JAYCE

JAYCE: WHERE ARE WE GOING, DADDY?

JAKE: IT'S UP TO YOU, USE YOUR IMAGINATION. WE CAN GO ANYWHERE YOUR MIND TAKES US.

JAYCE: LET'S GO TO THE JUNGLE!

JAKE: OK, THE JUNGLE IT IS!

JAKE & JAYCE

JAKE: OK JAYCE, WE HAVE TO JUMP THE WAY THEY DO IN THE MOVIES, THEN WE'LL LAND IN THE JUNGLE AND FIND SOME OF YOUR FAVORITE ANIMALS.

JAYCE: I'M READY TO FLY LIKE A SUPERHERO, DADDY! LET'S GO!

JAKE & JAYCE

JAYCE: LOOK, DADDY! THOSE MONKEYS ARE EATING ICECREAM, OUR FAVORITE SNACK.

JAKE: YOU SHOULD ASK THEM WHERE THEY GOT IT FROM, SO WE CAN GET SOME FOR OURSELVES.

JAYCE: HEY, MR. MONKEY! WHERE DID YOU GET THAT ICE CREAM FROM?

JAKE & JAYCE

JAYCE: DADDY, I'M GOING TO BUY BOTH OF US ONE WITH THE MONEY I SAVED.

JAKE: THANKS, JAYCE! I TOLD YOU ALL OF THAT SAVING WOULD PAY OFF. WHAT FLAVOR ARE YOU GETTING? I'M GOING WITH COOKIES AND CREAM.

JAYCE: I'M GOING TO GET HALF CHOCOLATE AND HALF VANILLA. I LOOOOVE ICE CREAM!

ICE CREAM
$1.00

JAKE & JAYCE

JAKE: ON TO THE NEXT PLACE, JAYCE!

JAYCE: LET'S GO, DAD. WATCH ME POP A WHEELIE!

JAKE: BE CAREFUL, JAYCE!

JAYCE: WOAHHH!

JAKE & JAYCE

JAKE: WAIT HERE, JAYCE. I'M GOING TO GO INSIDE TO GET YOUR MOTORCYCLE.

JAYCE: ARE YOU SCARED, DADDY? THERE MIGHT BE A BIG MONSTER IN THERE!

JAKE: I'M NOT SCARED OF ANYTHING! WHATEVER'S IN THERE BETTER BE SCARED OF ME!

JAKE & JAYCE

JAKE: JAYCE, THINK FAST!

JAYCE: HEY! PICK ON SOMEONE YOUR OWN
SIZE! (JAYCE THROWS STICK TO STOP THE
DINOSAUR)

JAKE & JAYCE

JAKE: THIS BADGE IS FOR BEING QUICK ON YOUR TOES AND SAVING MY LIFE. YOU'RE A BRAVE LITTLE GUY, JAYCE!

JAYCE: THANKS, DADDY! I'M GOING TO WEAR THIS EVERYDAY AND LET EVERYONE KNOW WHAT HAPPENED TODAY.

JAKE & JAYCE

JAKE: IT'S GETTING LATE. IS THERE ANY OTHER ANIMAL YOU WANT TO SEE BEFORE WE LEAVE THE JUNGLE?

JAYCE: YES, I HAVE A GREAT IDEA, DADDY. YOU'RE GOING TO LIKE THIS ONE, FOLLOW ME!

JAKE & JAYCE

JAYCE: IF WE CLIMB THIS BIG, BIG TREE, WE CAN SEE ALL THE ANIMALS IN THE JUNGLE AT ONE TIME!

JAKE: GREAT PLAN, JAYCE! BUT THIS IS A BIG TREE, YOU SURE YOU'RE NOT SCARED?

JAYCE: NO WAY! YOU TAUGHT ME NOT TO BE SCARED OF ANYTHING! COME ON, DADDY! HURRY!

JAKE & JAYCE

JAYCE: DADDY, I HAD THE BEST DREAM EVER! IT WAS SO COOL. WE JUMPED OUT OF A PLANE, WENT TO THE JUNGLE AND SAW ALL THE COOL ANIMALS. THEN WE GOT ICE CREAM FROM THE POLAR BEARS AND YOU ALMOST GOT EATEN BY A BIG DINOSAUR, BUT I SAVED YOU!

JAKE: WOW, JAYCE! THAT SOUNDS LIKE A GREAT DREAM BUT ALWAYS REMEMBER, DREAMS DO COME TRUE!

JAKE & JAYCE

WHAT DREAMS DO YOU WANT TO COME TRUE?

1. _____

2. _____

3. _____

4. _____

5. _____

CPSIA information can be obtained
at www.ICGtesting.com
Printed in the USA
LVHW070843080419
613336LV00012B/103/P

* 9 7 8 1 7 2 0 3 4 8 1 9 1 *